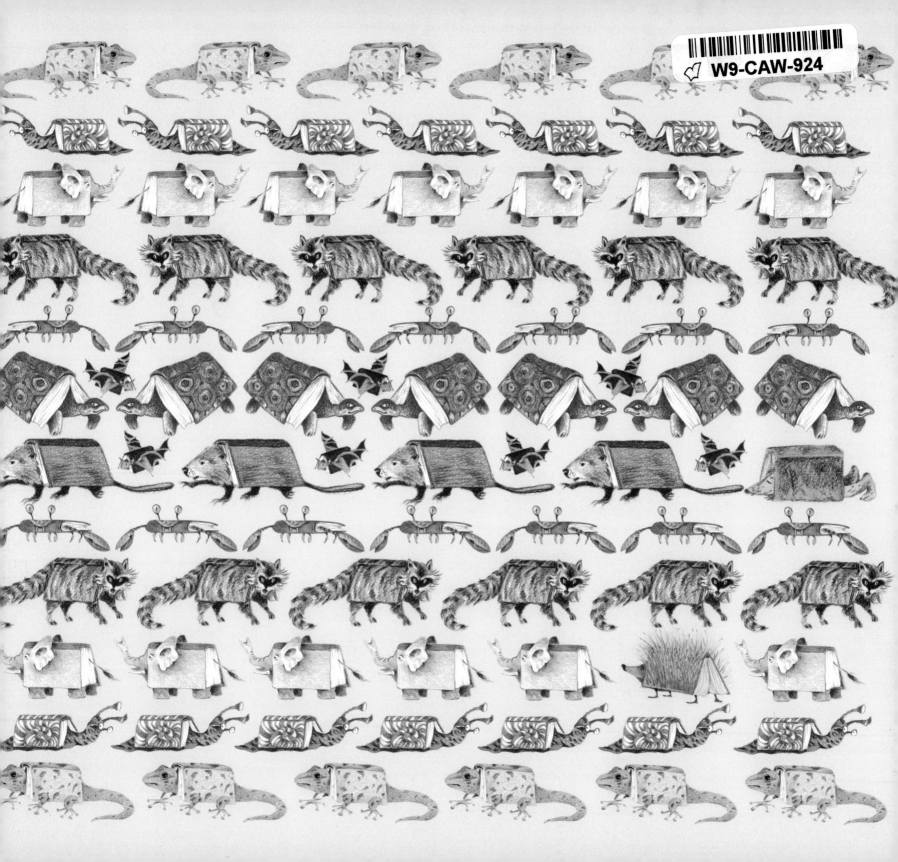

First Edition: March 2017

10 9 8 7 6 5 4 3 2 1

Printed in China

BREATHING BOOKS

Please write your name into this book and read it until the pages come loose. Leave your fingerprints in it and kiss its pages and fill it with life and memories, for that's what it wants!

Cornelia Funke

The Book
No One Ever Read

This is the story of Morry, a book who has been waiting...

Every book longs
to tell its story.

From the moment
they're bound,
they wait for fingers to
open them up.

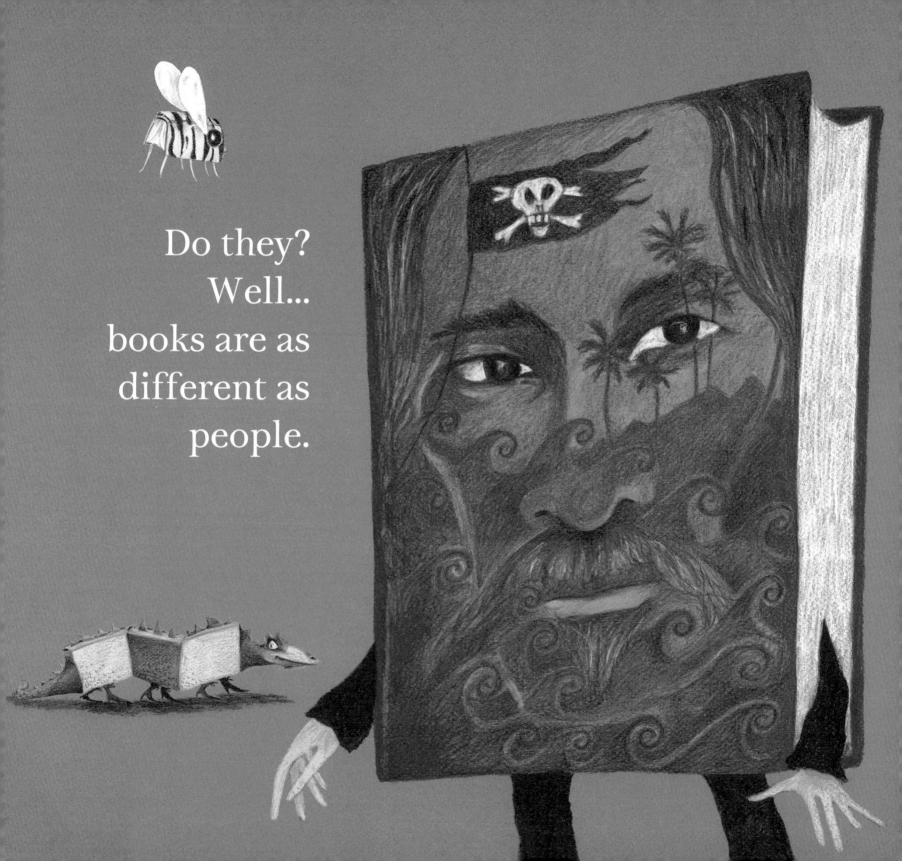

Do they?
Well...
books are as
different as
people.

Some are
adventurers
and want many
readers.

While others
have forgotten
they once longed
to tell their stories.

The library Morry lived in
was full of such books.
Morry was only five years old.
That is very young for a book.
But he thought that five years
are an awfully long time
to just sit on a shelf!

So one day
he pushed himself forward...
just a few inches.

"And where do you think you're going?" asked Victor.

He was very proud of the gold on his spine.

"Yes, what are you doing?" asked Jane.

"But I'm bored!" Morry exclaimed.
"No one ever reads us!"

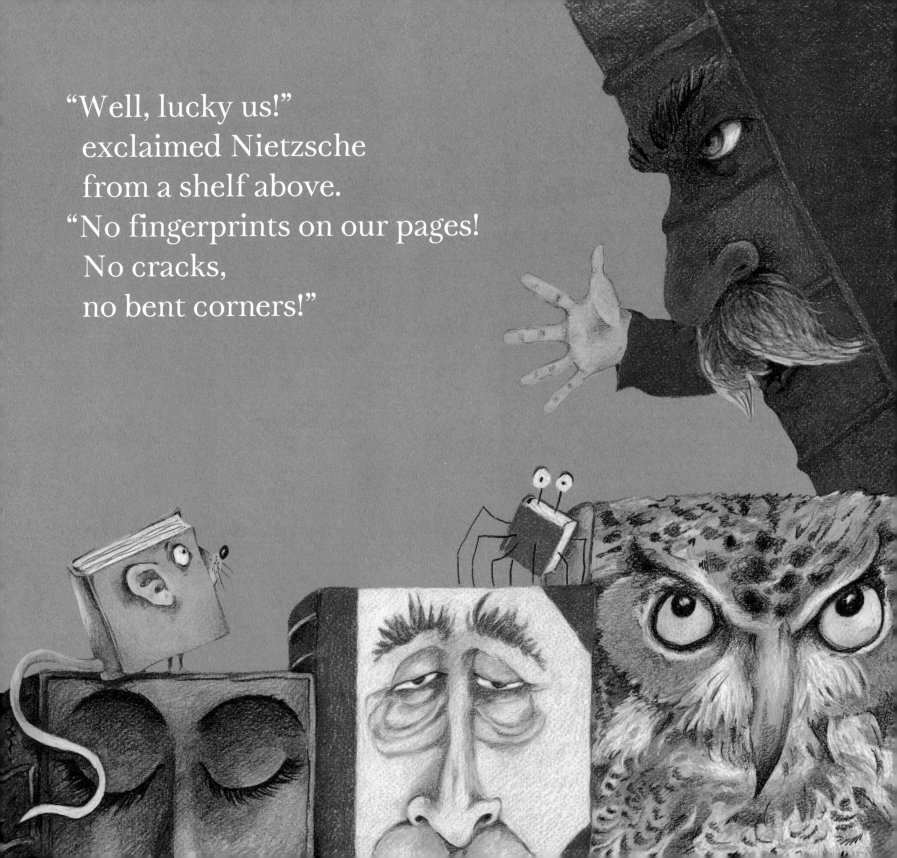

"Well, lucky us!"
exclaimed Nietzsche
from a shelf above.
"No fingerprints on our pages!
No cracks,
no bent corners!"

"Yes!" whispered Beatrix.
"One hears terrible things!
Books left open for days and
days, weeks even..."

She went on and on...
"Pages smeared with coffee
and chocolate!"

The others moaned after each sentence.

"Okay, that's terrible!"
said Morry.

"But not as terrible as
NOTHING HAPPENS! EVER!
I want fingerprints on my pages!
I want to be read, until I come apart!"

Oh, the moaning and rustling
that filled the library!

"Quiet, all of you!"
  shouted Dumas,
  who claimed you could learn fencing
  just by reading him.
"The young one is right!
  I would love to leave!
  But I am so old,
  I guess my spine would come off!"

"Leave?"
  asked Morry.
"How?"

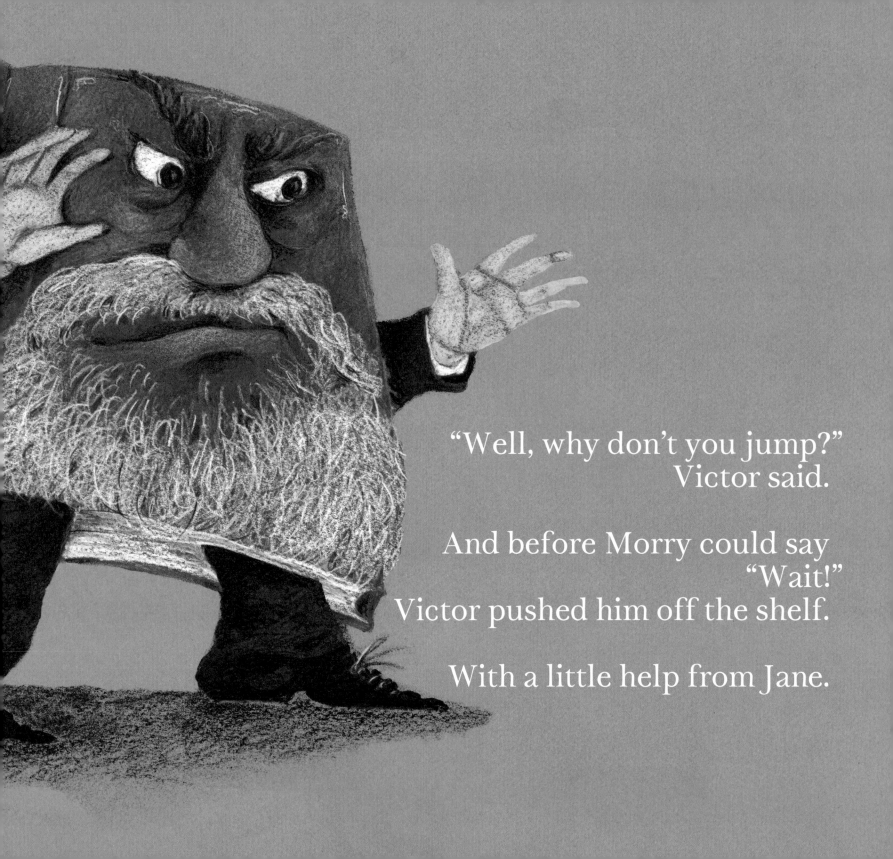

"Well, why don't you jump?"
Victor said.

And before Morry could say
"Wait!"
Victor pushed him off the shelf.

With a little help from Jane.

Luckily, Morry landed on his back.

The other books stared down
at him in horror.

Well, actually some of them
looked quite pleased.

And just when Morry got up,
the woman who dusted their
pages walked in!

Morry gathered all his courage
and slipped through the door.

Freedom!

Morry ran...and ended up on top of a huge staircase.

He stepped closer
when something furry
jumped at him.
Something furry with claws.

And Morry fell.

He fell down all the stairs.

Oh, it hurt.

He landed in front of two slippers.
And suddenly there were fingers and eyes.

The fingers were slightly sticky
but oh, it was wonderful!

The fingers wrote a name
on Morry's first page,

and the eyes read all the words
he'd kept for so long inside.

And Morry was soooo happy.

In honor of all the authors on whose books I left fingerprints, and read until their spines fell out, thank you Maurice Sendak, Shel Silverstein, Arundhati Roy, Robert Louis Stevenson, Mark Twain, Shaun Tan, Frank L. Baum, Victor Hugo, Jane Austen, Toni Morrison, Friedrich Nietzsche, Beatrix Potter, Alexandre Dumas, Astrid Lindgren, Shakespeare, Hugh Lofting, Friedrich Schiller, George Elliot, and many others who enchanted my life.